Princess Peppa
and the Royal Ball

Adapted by Courtney Carbone

SCHOLASTIC INC.

ISBN 978-1-338-18258-3

10 9 8 7 6 5 4 3 2   17 18 19 20 21

Printed in the U.S.A.   40
First Scholastic printing 2017
Book design by Jessica Meltzer

This is Princess Peppa.

Princess Peppa is excited.
Her family is having a ball at
the castle tonight!

Queen Mummy Pig and King Daddy Pig need help getting ready.

There is so much to do before the party!

"Can I invite my friends to the
ball?" asks Princess Peppa.
"Of course!" says Queen Mummy.

Princess Peppa and Prince
George go to the village.

Princess Peppa invites her
friends to the ball.

"Hooray!" they cheer.
Everyone can come.

Back at the castle, Grandpa
Wizard is getting the ballroom
ready. Princess Peppa wants to help!

Grandpa Wizard uses his magic
to make decorations appear
from Princess Peppa's broom.

Oh, no!
Some of the candles went out.
Princess Peppa asks for help
from a friendly dragon.

Next, Princess Peppa helps
King Daddy choose flowers for
the tables.

They pick the best ones from
the royal garden.

Princess Peppa brings the
flowers inside.
"Thank you, Peppa! These
are very pretty," says Queen
Mummy.

"Why don't you check on the desserts?" she asks Princess Peppa.

Peppa goes to the kitchen.
"What would you like to try?"
the royal baker asks.

"Everything, please!" Princess
Peppa says.
This is the best job so far.

The ballroom is ready.
The food is ready.
Everything is ready except
Princess Peppa!

She goes up to her room to change for the party.

Ring! It is the doorbell.
The guests are here!

Princess Peppa welcomes them to her royal ball.

A royal trumpet plays.
Prince George arrives in the
ballroom.

Queen Mummy and King Daddy
follow.
Now the royal ball can begin!

Everyone sings and dances
along to the music.

They eat yummy cakes and cookies.

"Thank you for making the
royal ball so special, Princess
Peppa," Queen Mummy says.

"And so yummy!" King Daddy
says.

They all danced happily ever after!